SACRAMENTO PUBLIC LIBRARY
828 "I" Street
Sacramento, CA   95814
3/10

CAST AWAY

WITHDRAWN FROM COLLECTION
OF SACRAMENTO PUBLIC LIBRARY

D1040936

This edition published 2008
First published 2000 by
A & C Black Publishers Ltd
38 Soho Square, London, W1D 3HB

www.acblack.com

Text copyright © 2000 Caroline Pitcher
Illustrations copyright © 2000 Peter Dennis
Cover illustration copyright © 2008 Anthony Williams

The rights of Caroline Pitcher and Peter Dennis to be
identified as author and illustrator of this work respectively
have been asserted by them in accordance with the
Copyrights, Designs and Patents Act 1988.

ISBN 978-0-7136-8572-5

A CIP catalogue for this book is available
from the British Library.

All rights reserved. No part of this publication may be
reproduced in any form or by any means – graphic, electronic
or mechanical, including photocopying, recording, taping or
information storage and retrieval systems – without the
prior permission in writing of the publishers.

This book is produced using paper that is made from wood
grown in managed, sustainable forests. It is natural, renewable and
recyclable. The logging and manufacturing processes conform to
the environmental regulations of the country of origin.

Printed and bound in China by C&C Offset Printing.

CAST AWAY

Caroline Pitcher

illustrated by Peter Dennis

A & C Black • London

CHAPTER ONE

It was dark outside. The sea boomed, and the wind whined around the window, as if it were looking for a way in. I could hear Laura snoring on the top bunk. Then Yasmin grabbed my arm.

Someone's outside!

She was right. The knob rattled.

I had to see who was there. The door creaked open. The corridor was dark, but there was a shape that seemed blacker than night. I could hear soft breathing.

Who is it?

Then someone whispered...

I want to talk to Laura.

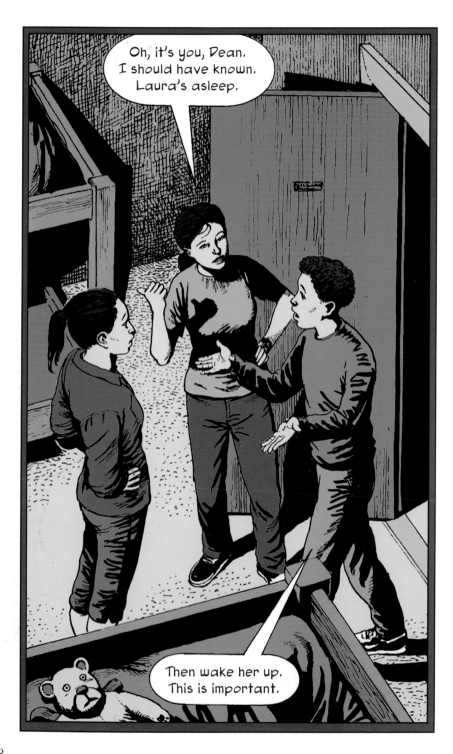

9

10

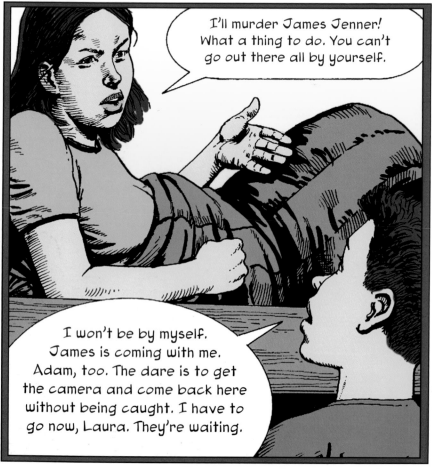

He blew Laura a kiss and was gone. Laura jumped out of her bunk and pulled on some clothes.

I looked at Yasmin, who gave me one of her "I told you so" looks.

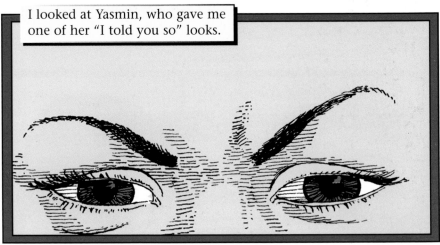

I sighed and began to pack my backpack.

15

CHAPTER TWO

In the distance, the sea churned and boomed. I thought it sounded like a giant washing machine. A full moon hung in the sky and bathed the wet beach in silver. Three eerie lights were bobbing and weaving ahead of us.

Suddenly a bright circle of light shone right in my face.

Stop it, James!

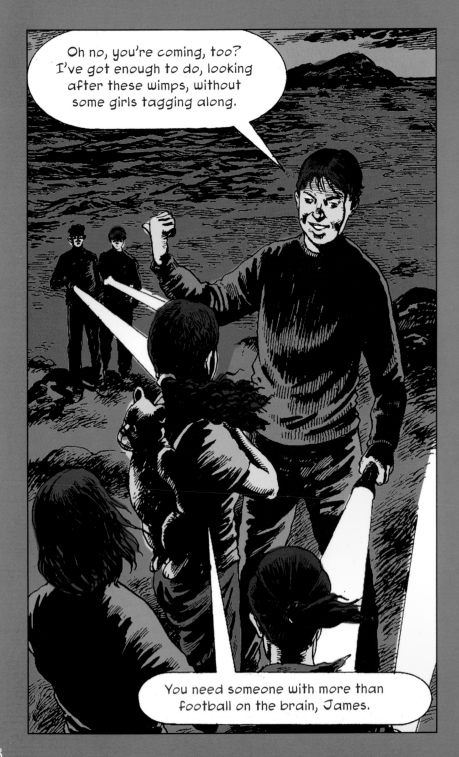

It wasn't really called Skull Island. That was James' idea. He'd named it Skull Island that morning. Its real name was East Rock. It was bleak though – just a heap of old rocks, gleaming pale and smooth and skull-like in the moonlight. You could only reach the island when the tide was out.

No one spoke. I glanced back at my footprints. They quickly vanished in the wet sand. They'd vanish soon, anyway, when the sea came up again.

We'd better hurry. It won't be long before the tide starts coming in...

What's that noise?

21

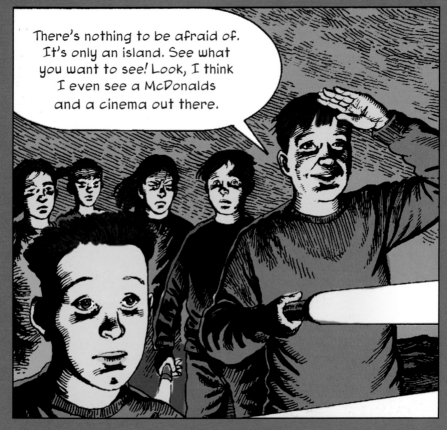

23

24

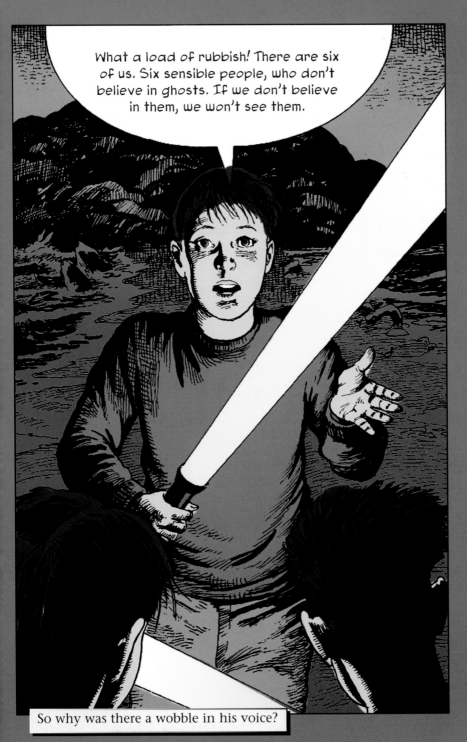

CHAPTER THREE

Yasmin tucked her arm in mine. She was shivering.

I don't like this, any of this.

Don't worry. We just have to make sure that Lean Mean Dean gets his stupid camera from the top of the rocks. Then we can go back and get into our nice, hard bunk beds.

But what if Miss Stephens and Mr Williams find out we're missing?

Dean didn't look too keen.

He was smiling. Now, I must tell you something. I used to be big friends with James Jenner. Just for a little while. But he boasts. He shows off. And he always has to have the last word.

We shone our torches on the rocks as Dean began to climb. In the moonlight, the rocks glistened. They must have been wet from the spray.

Not much of a mountain goat, are you, Dean?

Dean kept slipping and sliding, and stones tumbled from beneath his feet.

He's silly, climbing in trainers.

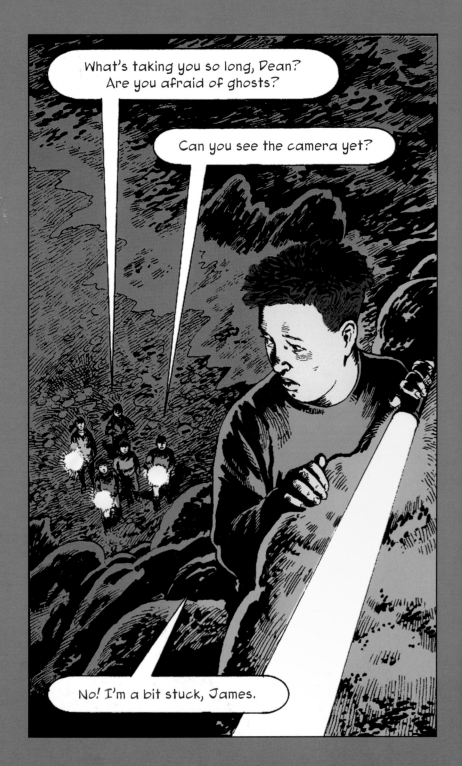

Yasmin says that they competed all the time when they were younger, James and Dean. Big sigh from James. He seemed to think he was in some kind of film, a hero, with a white vest and leather wrist bands with studs.

Go on, then, Macho Man Jenner. You do it!

All right, then, I will!

And then it happened. James lost his grip and did a kind of floppy-armed dance for a second. He looked like a crazy scarecrow.

Then he fell...

He took a long time to come down. He slipped and slithered and snatched at a clump of flowers, but it was no use.

He couldn't stop until he landed at the bottom.

It's all right. You're all right.

I heard myself saying this. How stupid I sounded! I was thinking concussion, punctured lung, broken back, tangled-up intestines...

It's all right, James, really.

But I knew it wasn't all right at all...

CHAPTER FOUR

Give me your phone, Adam.

Speechless, he handed me his mobile.

999 and our troubles will be over. James will be with a doctor before you can say "paramedic".

The phone wouldn't work.

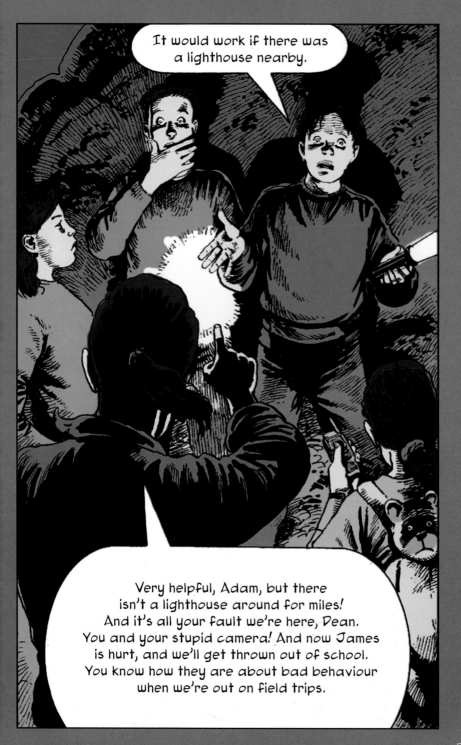

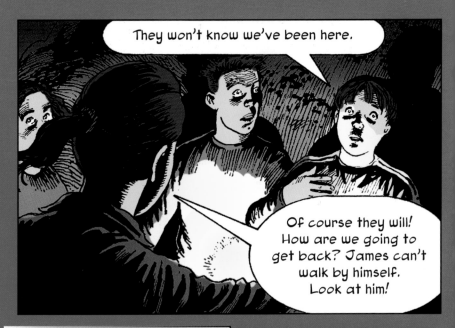

James was groaning and squirming around, and clutching his leg.

The sea had slid secretly, swiftly around the island and over the sands. We were cut off.

Adam snatched the whistle from Yasmin and blew it as hard as he could, again and again. But the wind just picked up the sound and carried it out to sea.

We'd seen puffins, cormorants, and terns.

We'd paddled in rock pools, like children, finding anemones and crabs.

We'd even built a sandcastle and had such a laugh.

It seemed like years ago. And now we were cast away, and no one knew.

How high does the tide come? We'll all be drowned!

CHAPTER FIVE

I ran back to warn the others. But they'd all gone! There was only James, lying on the rocks, moaning and muttering to himself.

I could hear my voice getting squeaky with panic. James shrugged and then winced. I felt mean. After all, he was in pain.

Then I heard something horrible…

I remembered Limpet Stores (with the E and T falling off its sign). I remembered buying shellfish and sweet, pink rock. I'd love to be outside Limpet Stores now!

So one of us was sick, another had disappeared, and the third couldn't walk. What about the other two, Dean and Laura?

I stared toward the distant shore of the mainland. There were two people in the sea. They were holding hands, as they waded out into the water.

They didn't hear me. As I watched, one of them suddenly vanished under the water!

CHAPTER SIX

The water was so cold it stopped my breath. How could it have got so deep so quickly? And the current was so strong! It swelled and shifted, and wanted to drag my legs away!

I heard my blood pounding in my ears as I struggled toward them, in slow motion. Suddenly, my feet left the bottom, and I was adrift!

Get control, girl!

I swam as strongly as I could...

...and came up next to Laura's terrified face.

Dean's face burst out of the water.

Dean coughed and spluttered and part of me wanted to laugh.

From somewhere in the back of my brain, I remembered the life-saving stuff that I'd learned years ago. But we saved lives in a swimming pool, not the North Sea.

Water surged over my face, and left me with sea in my mouth and lungs.

I'm not going to make it. I don't know which way to go.

At once I felt better. James' voice helped me focus on where I was going.

Never did a few minutes last so long. It seemed like five years later when the three of us collapsed on the shore.

I crawled over to James and pulled at my backpack. My numb fingers fumbled with the buckles.

I've still got my disgusting packed lunch.

t looked delicious now, that soggy bread illed with tuna mayonnaise. There were couple of spongy brown apples, a black banana, and some deformed chocolate biscuits. ames had squashed them with his big head. ike me, Laura and Dean were shivering.

He sounded so hopeful.

I took an extra huge bite into the sandwich. It was disgusting, but it was food. Poor James watched hungrily.

Thank you for calling out to me, James. I didn't know which way to go, so I just followed your voice until I was safe! I'm sorry you can't have anything to eat, really I am.

What's happened to Adam and Yasmin? There should be six of us, not four.

57

CHAPTER SEVEN

All right, we shouldn't have moved James. But what were we supposed to do? Leave him to drown as the water rose? He whimpered as we lifted him, and my heart flipped. I didn't like to hear him in pain. It hurt me, too.

Adam appeared from behind the rocks.

How should I know?
Have you got any bright ideas?
How about a hot air balloon? Or we can put a message in a bottle.
We haven't got a bottle.
Don't remind me how thirsty I am!
Did anyone else see that lightning?
That's all we need.

I hadn't heard any thunder, but then there was another flash, which made us jump. I hate storms. They frighten me, and I was frightened enough already.

Does anyone know where Yasmin is?

The others just shrugged.

I'm going to find her. You lot stay here.

There's not much else we can do, Kate!

61

I was careful as I climbed. Very careful. Soon I was at the top of the rock. I didn't dare stand up. I thought of home, of Mum and Dad, Jonathan and Sarah, and our cat, Chester, all sitting on the sofa, watching TV and eating chocolate biscuits. I felt so alone…

And then guess what I heard? Sad, sorrowful cries. Haunting, lost cries. They're seagulls, I told myself.

And then I looked at the waves. My heart skipped a beat.

Ghosts!

A hand touched my shoulder...

Kate, I was just coming back to find you.

I could have strangled her.

Yasmin! Where have you been?

What are those things?

Lots of them, aren't there?
Yes! But I don't want them to be there! I don't like ghosts!
Good, because they're seals. And that means there are fish, which probably means there are fishing boats. Do you know what we can do, Kate?

How could she be so calm? Hadn't she noticed the lightning?
I prayed she was right. I waved the torch around and
flashed it on and off, trying to remember Morse code.

And then it went out.
The battery was flat.

CHAPTER EIGHT

And then I saw it. It must have been there all along. It looked like a rock, a short distance away, because it was upside down.

Between us, we turned it over. Inside lay a pair of oars! And it looked just big enough for six. Yasmin grunted as she tried to move it.

The five of us carefully carried the boat down to the water.

We lifted James into the boat. He lay on the bottom. Then we scrambled in ourselves.

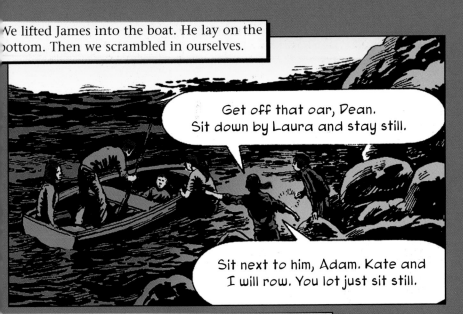

And so we rowed and rowed! We were going with the tide, and the storm seemed to have died away as soon as it started, so it wasn't too much of a struggle.

Our spirits rose as we neared the mainland.

But she spoke too soon...

70

Now I knew why that little boat had been abandoned on the island. It had a big hole in it! The boat was filling with water, and we were sinking fast.

CHAPTER NINE

But we didn't drown. By the time our
little boat sank, we were in shallow water.

It's all right!
My oar's just touched the bottom!

We carried James back to the cabin.

It's almost midnight!

The door isn't locked!

We sneaked in and struggled up the stairs. We
had all agreed to hide our dirty, wet clothes in our
backpacks. We were going home today anyway.

Laura, Yasmin and I had just changed into dry
clothes when we heard voices from the boys' room.

What do you mean, you fell out of bed?

I fell off the top bunk, sir. I was er - being - er -

Tarzan? A gorilla? What?

No, sir! I was making a save. Er - playing football. Yes, that's it. Dean tried to score a goal with his wash bag.

Mr Williams stared at them. Dean turned red in the face. We were standing behind Miss Stephens in the doorway. Mr Williams and Miss Stephens exchanged looks.

I don't believe them, do you?

James looked at me with a question in his brown eyes – "what do you think of me now?" I smiled. I was so pleased he was back safely. He winked a cheesy James wink. He must be feeling better.

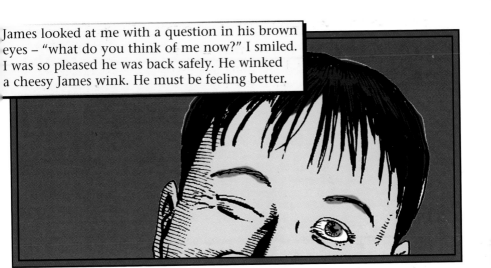

I wanted to kick Dean. All that terrible time, and we'd come through it without getting caught, and now he had to open his great, big mouth. I almost shouted at him that we only went out to Skull Island because of him. Well, all right, a lot of it was James' fault… Good thing I didn't say that. It would have given the whole game away.

Dean's mouth hung open, as Yasmin
dangled the camera in front of him.

So *that's* what she had been doing.
Everyone else had forgotten about the dare.

That's what the lightning was — the flash from the camera! No wonder I didn't hear any thunder.

Yasmin's smile was full of mischief and delight. Everyone else, Dean and Laura and Adam and James, simply looked stunned. Their expressions changed as they realised what she had done. Then they were furious!

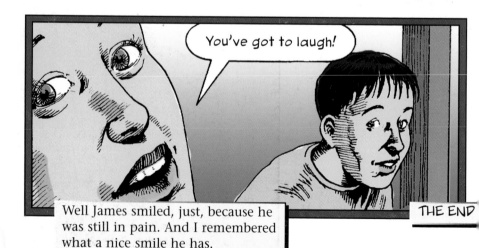

Well James smiled, just, because he was still in pain. And I remembered what a nice smile he has.

THE END